Wag and the King

For my brother Alan – One Man
and His Dogs

Tales from the Keep

Wag and the King

Joan Lennon   Scoular Anderson

Catnip

CATNIP BOOKS
Published by Catnip Publishing Ltd
14 Greville Street
London EC1N 8SB

First published 2009
1 3 5 7 9 10 8 6 4 2

Text copyright © Joan Lennon 2009
Illustrations copyright © Scoular Anderson 2009
The moral rights of the author and illustrator have been asserted

A CIP catalogue record for this book is available from the
British Library

ISBN 978-1-84647-065-3

Printed in Poland

www.catnippublishing.co.uk

Contents

Chapter One

Old Dog, New Tricks?

Remember that thing they say?

You can't teach an old dog new tricks.

Ever stop to wonder *why*? If you did, you probably thought it was because old dogs are too stupid, or old dogs are too stiff. Rubbish! Old dogs can't learn new tricks because *they haven't got the time!*

My name's Wag. I'm old, and I'm a dog. And I am SO BUSY keeping my human out of trouble that I have NO TIME LEFT to learn tricks. Old tricks, new tricks, tricks of *any* sort or smell.

Oh, come on, you say. No one can get in *that* much trouble, you say. You *must* be exaggerating.

That's what you say.

Are you right? I don't think so. Take last week, for example …

Chapter Two

Apprentice Tom

The Boy's name is Tom, and I've had him ever since his parents left him here, at the Castle, when he was little more than a puppy.

Do you know about apprenticing? If you do, you can skip the rest of this bit. If you don't – this is how it works.

Humans with a big litter apprentice some of them to other humans (called Masters) who are skilled at something the parents don't know much about themselves. The children learn a new trade by watching and helping and being taught, and the Master gets a new assistant. Even the Princes and Princesses get sent away to other castles, to learn things about Kinging and Queening that maybe their own mothers and fathers aren't so good on. It's a pretty sensible system, and mostly it all works out quite well.

Mostly.

In Tom's case, his parents apprenticed him to the Court Minstrel. On the face of it, they couldn't have chosen a better job for their son: no heavy lifting, indoor work, guaranteed invitations to every feast, nice clothes and a warm basket, er, bed to sleep in.

The Master Minstrel was one of the Old King's favourites. The Old King died not so long ago, and his son Roderick was called back from *his* apprenticeship to take over. So now we have a Young King. He's still new at the job and has a lot to learn, but he seems a likeable enough human. *And* he seems to be perfectly happy with his father's Minstrel, so that should be good news for the Boy, too.

It sounds great, doesn't it?

As it worked out, however, it was a bit like apprenticing a Jack Russell to an Irish Wolfhound.

Not exactly the perfect match, if you get what I mean.

Chapter Three

Minstrel Mismatch

"You CANNOT sing an Ode to the Beauty of Lady Gravel with your eyes crossed and pretending to be sick all the time!" the Master shouted.

"You cannot sing an Ode to the Beauty of Lady Gravel AT ALL!" the Boy shouted back. "Because the Beauty of Lady Gravel doesn't exist!!"

There you have it. It's not that our Tom can't sing – he has quite a nice voice, and we've had many a pleasant howl together of an evening. But when it comes to flattering the Lords and Ladies of the Court with flowery

phrases, or complimenting all the
Royal Relatives in rhyming couplets, or
warbling "The Lament of Lord Stush" –
well, as far as *that* part of the job goes,
the Boy hasn't the nose for it, and no
mistake.

19

The Lord, a-weltering in his blood,
Took a long last look at his Lady
And murmured "My Dearest,
oh my, ah me!
When I'm dead,
dear Lady,
remember me!"

And she looked at him,
and sighed and said,
"All right, but I really do
not suppose
That you're going to die,
With a slight black eye
And a great big fat
bloody nose!"

21

You get the idea.

In the course of this morning alone, the Boy had already had a scroll, a roll, and a flagon thrown at him by the Master.

"GET OUT GET OUT GET OUT!" bellowed the Master. "And take that mangy mongrel with you!"

Tom grinned at me. Escape! But then the Master changed his mind.

"NO!" he yelled. "Come back. I've got a better idea."

Uh-oh. The Boy and I exchanged worried looks.

"You can attend the King's Audience instead. And you can *stay there* until you find something *you* deem worthy of singing an Ode about. Don't come back without a finished song. And take the dog."

He could be really mean, the Master.

So there we were, stuck in the Great Hall, listening to a bunch of old poops droning on about drains and taxes and treaties and trade. The only person more bored than us was the Young King.

He kept yawning behind his hand, and playing with his sleeves. (Great long droopy sleeves-to-the-floor was one of the idiot fashions he'd brought back from his apprenticeship at Castle Finicky.) He looked really silly, and really fed up.

Until … there was a blare of trumpets that made everybody jump. They only use the trumpets to announce the arrival of *really important* people. So who important would want to show up to an event as dull as this one? I wondered.

I was just about to find out – and when I did, I couldn't stop my tail from wagging like a windmill.

Chapter Four

WOW!

What walked through those big double doors was an absolute vision of exotically-clipped fur, high-stepping paws, and the sweetest snout.

Oh, and the human with her wasn't bad either.

"The Lady Spectacula, Ambassadress from the Kingdom of Grimm," announced the Chamberlain in a disapproving voice. "Our long-standing rival. And enemy. And traditional adversary. Locally known as The Bad Guys."

The old Chamberlain was definitely

trying to
send a
message to
the Young
King, but
he wasn't
receiving.
Young
Roderick
was wearing
an utterly
goopy
expression
all over his
face. Even
Tom looked
a little

open-mouthed. It probably had to do with the way Lady Spectacula was dressed.

In my opinion, though, something didn't smell right about the Ambassadress, and it wasn't just her perfume. Unfortunately, the King only had a human nose.

"Silence, Chamberlain! How *dare* you be rude to this fair Lady!" he squeaked. Then he got his voice back under control. "You are all dismissed," he said, trying to sound like his father. "I will meet with the Ambassadress from Grimm – alone!"

Well, I wasn't going anywhere with a lady dog like that around, and the Boy was too curious to even consider leaving. So we slid out of sight together behind the throne, and waited while the

Great Hall reluctantly emptied.

At last there was a moment's silence,
and then a CLICK. We peeked.

The Lady had just finished locking
the big double doors, and was turning
round. She started slinking up the Hall
towards the King like some horrible
cat, smiling at him with a whole
mouth full of little white teeth. The

lady dog padded gracefully along at
her embroidered heels.

"Your Majesty," the Lady purred as
they came close. "Thank you so much.

For this opportunity to be alone with you and ..."

"Mnerg," gargled Roderick.

"... to END YOUR LIFE!"

31

You've never seen a dog – or a human – change so fast. All the sweetness disappeared, lost in snarls, as the two launched themselves at the King. The Lady had a knife in one hand – the lady dog had her jaws wide – the King threw himself backwards – we leaped out of hiding – and the result was a yelling, snapping scrum on the floor.

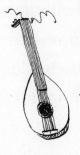

Chapter Five

Run! Run!

"*Look out!*"

"GRRRRRRR!!!!!!"

"DIE!! DIE!!"

"Grrrrr —YIP!"

"OWWWW!"

The attackers had evidently *not*
expected any company. Tom made
use of their confusion to tangle the
Grimmian dog up in the Lady's skirts,
while I managed to bite her on the
hand. The knife went flying – and then
so did we!

"This way, Your Majesty!" Tom
yelled, dragging the King by one arm

through the servant's door behind the throne. I could hear the Grimmians struggling to untangle themselves as we slammed it shut, as well as a faint cry of "*Come back, you coward!*"

"Run, Your Majesty!" Tom called over his shoulder as he piled some old boxes against the door to slow the assassins down.

But Roderick was just standing there, staring.

"I never knew there was a door there," he murmured, sounding dazed.

"Come ON!"

We'd barely gone three steps when the King fell over onto his nose. Tom helped him up, and then he was down again.

"Oh these *idiot* sleeves!" muttered the King as he tripped over them yet again.

"What I wouldn't give for some proper clothes and a sword …"

I couldn't do anything about the sword, but a dog is as good as his teeth.

RRRIPPPP!

"Great St Bernard! Even your dog's attacking me!"

RRRRRIIIIPPPPP!

I could hear the laughter – and exasperation – in Tom's voice.

"No, Your Highness. Wag's just, um, redesigning your costume. So you won't trip up so much. Or look so much like an idiot. Your Majesty. Sire."

The King spluttered. He was not used to all this, you could tell. Tom tucked the sleeves into his belt and set off again.

"Let's try along here!"

We raced down one of the back corridors, until Tom skidded to a stop.

"We'll hide in here," he said, "till the Guards catch up."

We piled into a disused cupboard. Luckily it was almost empty, because there certainly wasn't a lot of room in there for two humans and a dog. The King managed to crack his head on a shelf a few times, before he learned to stay low.

"Where *are* we?" he panted. "I thought I knew my own Castle! I certainly thought about it enough when I was away."

"You wouldn't know back here,
Your Highness, you being a Prince
and all. You'd just know the posh
bits. It's the servants and apprentices,
people like that, who *really* know
a castle." Tom was busy peering
through a crack in the door, so he
didn't see the look the King gave him.
But I did.

Young Roderick was *really* not used to all this.

"Where are the Guards?" muttered Tom. "Why haven't they shown up yet?"

The King turned pink.

"I expect they're still trying to break down the door of the Great Hall. She … locked it."

"And you let her."

"I … she … um …"

I whined and made a big thing of putting my nose to the floor. Tom stared at me for a minute, puzzled, and then slapped his forehead.

"Of course – we can't hide here! She'll be using that dog to track us! Come on!"

The King groaned, straightened up too soon, banged his head again, moaned, and then managed to drag himself out into the corridor after us. He'd acquired three cobwebs and an irate spider in his hair, and a generous smudging of dirt, all over.

You had to grin.

"Tell your dog to stop laughing at me," the King growled. "He's no picture of elegance, either."

But there was no time for chat.

I could smell them now – the lady dog and the killer Lady – getting dangerously close. Without a yip, I led the way.

"Where …?" I heard the King begin, but the Boy told him to Shush. And he didn't say Please.

I knew we had to get the Grimmians off our tails soon. I also knew we had to get help – there was *no chance* we could beat them in a straight fight.

Fortunately, I had a plan.

Chapter Six

What's That Smell?

"Ah-ha!" said Tom. "Who's a clever dog then?"

We'd arrived, and the Boy seemed to have caught on to my idea right off.

We exchanged glances, and started to move in behind Roderick. But the King didn't notice. He was too busy staring at the midden as if he'd never seen one before – come to think of it, he probably never had – and holding his nose.

"Where are we? What's that smell? What are we doing here? Wha – EEEK!!"

A shove from the Boy and a nip from

me, and the first part of the plan was accomplished. No dog on earth could distinguish the single scent of a King from all the smells of the midden.

"Lie still, Your Majesty," Tom hissed as he covered up the few bits of Monarch that still showed. "We'll be back for you as soon as the coast is clear!"

Then, dragging the King's ripped-off sleeves along the ground to lay a false trail, we were off again.

Round behind the kitchens, past the privy, under the washing-lines we went. Our pursuers were gaining on us. This old dog was panting and puffing, and even the Boy's young legs were starting to stumble.

"Nearly ... there ..." I heard him gasp.

Over some barrels, in one door and out another, round a corner – *and there it was!*

THE GUARDHOUSE!!

"Help! Guards! The King ..." yelled Tom with all the breath he had left.

I'll never forget the look on their faces as the Lady and her hound skidded round the last corner seconds later, and saw us ... just us and not a sniff of the King (unless you count a couple of draggled sleeves) – with a

dozen burly guardsmen on either side –
WOOF!!

The Guardsmen piled in, doing
guardsmanly things in a nervous sort
of way – you could tell they weren't
used to dealing with High-Class Female
Threats to the Monarchy, human *or*
dog. But still, in the end, they managed
to get the two bundled away.

And us? Well, for a while we just sat
there on the Guardhouse steps, in the
nice sun, with our tongues hanging out.
Then I noticed that the Boy's expression
was beginning to change. His face went
from looking all red and excited … to
looking uneasy … to looking pale and
worried sick.

"I can't believe I just shoved the King
in a cupboard, Wag," he muttered.

Yes, but you saved his life, I thought back.

"I can't believe you just ripped the King's sleeves off," he murmured.

Yes, but I saved his life, I thought again.

"I *really* can't believe we just pushed the King into the midden and covered him up with rubbish," he moaned.

Yes, but we really did save his life, I insisted.

Tom didn't hear.

"We are *so* in trouble," he groaned, and buried his head in his hands.

Which is why he didn't immediately see the Monster.

It appeared unannounced from around the corner, and slurped slowly towards us, leaving a trail of pungent vegetable bits in its wake. Potato peelings wreathed its head and shoulders; carrot tops stuck to its feet like seaweed; and strange unidentifiable smudges and stains coloured its body and face.

And then there was the smell …

"I take it 'the coast is clear,'" it said, in a very flat voice.

Tom's head jerked up.

"Y – Your Majesty," he stammered.

Ah, I thought, *not a Monster then.*

"If the … emergency is over, I would like to bathe," continued the Monster – I mean, Monarch. "Kindly inform my valet that I will be in my chambers."

Without waiting for an answer, King

Roderick turned, wetly, and glooped away.

"I am so dead," said Tom. If he'd had a tail, it would have drooped. He trudged off in search of the King's valet.

He seemed to want to be by himself for some reason, so I let him go. There wasn't anything more I thought I should be doing, so I turned myself around a few times, curled up, and went to sleep.

Chapter Seven

The Feast ...

Several days later, there was a feast
to honour the King's victory over the
Grimmian spy. Unfortunately, the
Master Minstrel had caught a bad cold
in the meantime, and lost his voice
almost completely. There was no way *he*
would be able to sing!

So that left ...

"Now remember what I've taught
you, Tom," croaked the Master. "Loud
clear voice, don't rush, and for goodness'
sake, make the King look good!"

He gave the Boy a shove. Tom stumbled
forward into the centre of the Great Hall

and stopped dead. The babble of voices carried on around him. He didn't speak. He didn't move. He looked frozen with fear.

There are some moments when a cold wet nose firmly applied to a human's hand is the only way to get them operational.

"AKKK!" squawked Tom. Not the most elegant opening, but at least it got everybody's attention.

The old Chamberlain rose to his feet and announced, "Your Majesty. Lords and Ladies. Due to the Master Minstrel's unfortunate illness, his apprentice will sing for us tonight, on the subject of King Roderick's Recent Heroic Victory Over the Evil Grimmian Assassin."

Another application of the cold-and-wet got the Boy strumming. As I looked around at the audience I could see a range of expressions, from complete indifference to polite interest. The King, of course, had had lots of practice not showing his feelings on his face, but I could see one of his feet under the table.

It was tapping nervously.

The Boy's voice was a bit wobbly, but it *was* loud, and more or less in tune.

"A minstrel's task is to tell the tale
Of the Mighty Deeds of the Great.
I'm here to sing, to one and all,
The dire events that did befall
Our Sovereign King in his Audience Hall
And ..."

He paused. He strummed a few chords, then nodded, as if he'd made up his mind about something. Then he began to sing again.

But there had been a change.

"… And the truth is what I'll tell."

The King's foot froze, and he sat
forward a little in his throne. All through
the Great Hall there was an uneasy
rustle of expensive clothes. But the Boy
didn't seem to notice. It was almost as if
he were singing to himself.

Then she lunged with her dagger!
The King leapt in the air
But - lucky for him! -
This Old Dog was still there!

57

As a rule, dogs don't blush. But when he said that, and everyone looked at me – well, I certainly got hot under the collar.

59

The Great Hall was so still you could have heard a flea hop. As the tale unfolded, there were open mouths wherever you looked, and the King was as pale as a bowl of milk.

That was the end. There was a moment of deeply, truly horrified silence after Tom stopped playing. Nobody breathed.

Then ...

"That's not the truth, you know," said the King quietly.

Chapter Eight

Fired!

A babble of voices exploded around us.

"Well of course it isn't the truth!"

"No one would believe such a thing!"

"The *idea*!"

"The boy should be flogged!"

"Outrageous!"

King Roderick raised his hand and the noise stopped short.

"I know it's not the truth," he continued, "because I was there. I *know* what happened. And I know it wasn't just the dog who saved me."

There was another, more uncertain pause. The courtiers were confused. But the King wasn't.

"It was *you* too," he said to Tom. "*That's* the truth." He raised his voice a little, to make sure that everyone could hear. "I was very, very stupid. And an apprentice boy and a dog saved my life."

His eyes hadn't left us.

"You could have made something

up, you know. To make me look good.
That's what minstrels are supposed to
do, isn't it? But you didn't. Why didn't
you? Is it because you don't like me? Or
don't you want to be a minstrel?"

The Boy scuffed his shoes about in
the rushes for a bit, and then muttered,

"I like the singing. And the stories.
I like telling stories. But – " and here

his voice got so quiet the King and
the entire Court had to lean forward
to hear him " – I like the stories to be
true."

There was another pause. Then the
elderly Chamberlain coughed.

"Yes, Chamberlain?" said the King
politely.

"I have a suggestion, Sire," the old
man wheezed.

The King nodded encouragingly.

"And my suggestion is this. Sack the apprentice minstrel. He obviously isn't fit for the job."

Tom's face fell; my tail drooped. He was going to be sent away! I'd never see him again!

But the old man wasn't finished.

"Give him a new job," he continued. "Let him be your Fool."

Some of the younger courtiers looked blank, but *I* remembered the

Old King's Fool. He'd been like an unofficial advisor for years, until he got too wobbly on his legs and went to live out his days in the country. He'd always dressed his advice up in wild jokes and stories. But I remember the Old King always listened …

"My what?" said the Young King.

"Your Fool, Sire. It's an old custom, having one person in Court who will always speak the truth to the powerful," the Chamberlain explained. "It doesn't mean he can just go about being rude, though. Oh no. His truth has to be dressed in stories and songs and jokes. But he has your permission *never to have to lie*. Oh, and he has to wear a special costume: a funny hat, and bells on his trousers, and a multi-coloured shirt, and he carries around a stick with lots of ribbons – that sort of thing."

"In other words, he gets to dress up like an idiot," laughed the King. Then he became serious again. "Would you like to do this, Tom? Would you like to be my Fool?"

I held my breath. *Don't go away, Boy!* I thought at him as hard as I could. *Take the job! Take the job!*

He put a hand on my head and gave me a long, serious look. Then he squared his shoulders, and spoke to the King.

"The answer is yes, Your Majes … Roderick. I would be happy to be your Fool. We both would – I, *and* Wag."

The King nodded solemnly.

"Of course," he said.

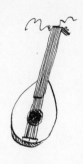

Chapter Nine

Old Dog, New Job

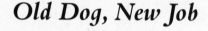

Well? I told you I wasn't exaggerating.
I really AM too busy just trying to keep
the Boy out of trouble. Learn new tricks,
ha! NO TIME.

But he's got this new job now, you
say. He can't possibly get into any more
trouble *now*.

That's what you say.

And I say …

PULL THE OTHER THREE –

THEY'VE GOT BELLS ON!

If you enjoyed Wag and the King you'll love the other books in the Tales from the Keep series.

The Ferret Princess

Princesses come in all shapes and sizes
– from pink and fluffy to ravishing and
regal, and everything else besides.

I'm the ferrety sort. I've got loads
more energy than sense and I just can't
help sticking my nose into things. Or
making a mess out of sheer enthusiasm.

But when two wicked princes arrived
looking for a kingdom to take over
I needed all my ferrety talents to see
them off – not to mention the help of
my very own ferrets!

Out now!

Tales from the Keep

Coming soon!

The Mucker's Tale

Read the opening chapter of the new
Tales from the Keep story now ...

Chapter One

The Wizard and the Sweeper Boy

The ragged boy leaned on his broom and sighed as the wizard walked past. Once again, he hadn't had the nerve to speak to the old man, to ask him the questions that filled his mind day and night …

KABOOM!

The wizard had just started up the steps to his magnificent house when the street shook and a cloud of smelly purple smoke billowed out of the front door. He turned around quickly and went back down again.

He noticed that a ragged boy with a broom was watching him, and he smiled.

"I think I'll just sit out on the steps for a bit, and let that settle," the wizard said to him. "Perhaps you'd like to join me?"

The ragged boy's eyes went very big, but he came over anyway and sat down beside the wizard.

"What's your name?" the old man asked. He was wearing a fabulously pointy hat and fancy robes and had a spectacularly long white beard, but he had a kind voice.

"They call me Sweeper, Honoured

Sir," the boy said. "Because that's my job. I sweep the streets."

The old man chuckled. "You know what they used to call me when I was your age?" he said. "Mucker!"

The boy couldn't believe it. "You mean – you weren't always a wizard?" he exclaimed.

"Oh no – not by a long shot! Once I was just a stable boy, and nobody called me 'Honoured Sir'! No, like I said, everybody called me 'Mucker'!"

And the wizard's mind went back to those long ago days and, as Sweeper listened, he began to tell a story …

Chapter Two

Kingdom in the Sky

"Hey, Mucker!"

Oh yes, that was me. I grew up in a tiny kingdom, hidden so high in the mountains that the clouds kept bumping into the castle walls. From as soon as I was tall enough to handle a broom, I'd been the stable boy.

The castle stable wasn't very big, but it still needed a lot of sweeping because, as you know, all horses are really, really good at producing manure. And once it's been produced, somebody has to muck it all out, and that somebody was me.

I didn't mind. Not too much, anyway.
Because the horses I was sweeping up
after weren't just ordinary horses. Not
by a long shot. Our horses could fly.

You don't see flying horses much
outside the mountains. They are
creatures of the cold, feeding on
meadow grass and pine trees and
thriving in the frigid air. Also, although
they can take off from a flat running
start, they much prefer a decent
launching cliff to get airborne, and they
are at their best with the kind of savage
winds that batter round mountain peaks
like ours.

You might say I was really lucky,
getting to work with such fabulous

animals. And I was! But the problem was, there was something I wanted to do even more.

I wanted to be a wizard.

And I wasn't the only one.

Even though our kingdom was small and out of the way, it still had everything a kingdom should have. We had an extremely honourable King (who was, sadly, a widower), a collection of Courtiers, some Faithful Old Retainers, the bravest of brave Guardsmen, a deliciously talented Cook, a Court Wizard (whose name was "Magnus the Magnificent") ... and a Princess. Her name was Emmeline.

You might say she was really lucky, too, being a Princess. But there was something she wanted to be doing, even more than princessing, just like me. She wanted to be a wizard too.

We used to meet up in the stables and complain about our lives. (Emmeline was as good with the flying horses as I was. She would practise her singing on them and brush the gunk out of their tails and lend a hand when my two just weren't enough. She was also teaching me to read, as I had no time for proper schooling.)

"My father makes me take singing lessons and history lessons and algebra lessons, but he won't let me take lessons from Magnus the Magnificent," moaned Emmeline. "He says princesses don't need to know how to do magic."

"Same here," I moaned back. "Stable

boys don't need to know how to do magic either."

"I don't think he'll ever change his mind," sighed Emmeline. "Nothing ever changes around here."

"Nothing ever changes, and nothing ever happens," I sighed back.

And it really did feel like that. It felt as if everything would stay just the way it was for at least a hundred million years. Until, one day, something did happen, and everything changed.

That was the day the raiders came …

Joan Lennon

About Joan Lennon ...
Joan Lennon was born in Toronto in
Canada and now lives in Scotland.
She is married with four tall sons and
one short, fat cat. As well as the
Tales from the Keep stories, she has
written *Questors*, *The Seventh Tide* and
The Wickit Chronicles.

Those are the facts, but here's the
story ...

Once upon a time a little girl was
born in a strange and far off land called
Canada. She had a mummy, a daddy,
a big sister with beautiful curly long
blonde hair (with whom she had to
share a bedroom) and a big brother
who kept snakes and didn't have to
share his bedroom with anybody, not
even them. The little girl, by the way,

did not have beautiful curly long blonde hair. She had very ordinary straight short brown hair. There are many things in life that are not at all fair.

Under the circumstances, there was nothing for this little girl to become but a spy. Sadly, her knees made cracking noises when she tried to sneak up behind anybody, so she decided instead to become a writer.

As the years passed, Canada started to not seem nearly strange and far off enough, so the little girl (who was now as grownup as she was likely to become) tried some other countries. She had a go at Germany, and Australia, and Yugoslavia, and England, and Wales, and Scotland. The last one was the best, and to this day, you will find her there, happily writing books, but still cracking her knees nostalgically from time to time at the thought of what might have been.

www.joanlennon.co.uk